Good books are some of the greatest treasures in the world. They can take you to incredible places and on fantastic adventures. So sit back with a **10 MINUTE CLASSIC** and indulge a lifelong love for reading.

We cannot, however, guarantee your 10 minute break won't turn into 15, 20, or 30 minutes, as these FUN stories and engaging pictures will have you turning the pages AGAIN and AGAIN!

Designed by Flowerpot Press
in Franklin, TN.
www.FlowerpotPress.com
Designer: Stephanie Meyers
Editor: Katrine Crow
DJS-0912-0166
ISBN: 978-1-4867-1222-9
Made in China/Fabriqué en Chine

KING
Sir Thomas Malory
ARTHUR
The Story of How Arthur Became King

10 Minute Classics

Retold by
Philip Edwards

Illustrated by
Adam Horsepool

Sometimes the world needs someone special. How that someone is found is often a mystery. King Arthur's tale is not one of mystery. When the world needed Arthur it found him in a magical way, such had never been seen before or since...

3

Once upon a time, a thousand years before Christopher Columbus sailed to America and when Rome was still the greatest city in the world, there lived a brave and handsome young man named Arthur. He hailed from a town not far from London, where he lived in a castle with his father, Sir Ector, and his older brother, Sir Kay.

Arthur liked to lie under the trees and gaze up at the sky. All about him stood old oaks, like giant guardians watching sturdily over the soil where they had grown for centuries. Arthur loved listening to the magic of the forest; rabbits and squirrels whisking about, a herd of brown deer with shy dark eyes passing by, or a flock of pheasants with brilliant plumage rising from the bushes. Sometimes there was no sound at all except the fluttering of leaves or the trembling of violets half buried in green moss. In the solitude of the woods, Arthur would dream of one day becoming a noble knight.

When Arthur wasn't daydreaming in the woods, he spent many hours of the day training to become a knight. Arthur learned to hunt, carry a lance properly, and use a sword skillfully. As was common for knights in training, Arthur dutifully served his brother and father as a squire. He was given important tasks, such as caring for their armor and accompanying them to tournaments. These skills all combined to teach young squires the principles of knighthood: service, courtesy, and humility. Arthur notoriously surpassed his fellow squires in all attributes and was known as the most humble, respectful, and hardworking of them all.

At this time there was no ruler in Britain. The powerful King Uther, who had governed the people of Britain, had died years earlier, and all the strong lords of the country were struggling to be king in his place. This gave rise to a great deal of quarreling and bloodshed.

Fortunately, there was in the land a wise magician named Merlin. He was so old that his beard was as white as snow, but his eyes were as clear as a young child's. He was known across the land for his mystical abilities and many looked to him for wisdom and guidance. Merlin was very sorry to see all the fighting because he feared it would do serious harm to the kingdom.

In those days, the great and good men who
ruled in the church had power almost equal to
that of the monarch.* Merlin went to the Archbishop of
Canterbury, the churchman who in all of Britain was the most
beloved, and said, "Sir, it is my advice that you send to all the great
lords of the realm and bid them come to London by Christmas
to choose a king."

The archbishop did as Merlin advised, and at Christmas all the great
lords came to London. There were so many of them that they quite filled
the entire cathedral. The good archbishop looked at their stern bronzed faces,
their heavy beards, their broad shoulders, and their glittering armor, and he

*Monarch is another name for a person who rules a kingdom.

Whosoever pulls this sword from this stone and anvil is the true King of all Britain.

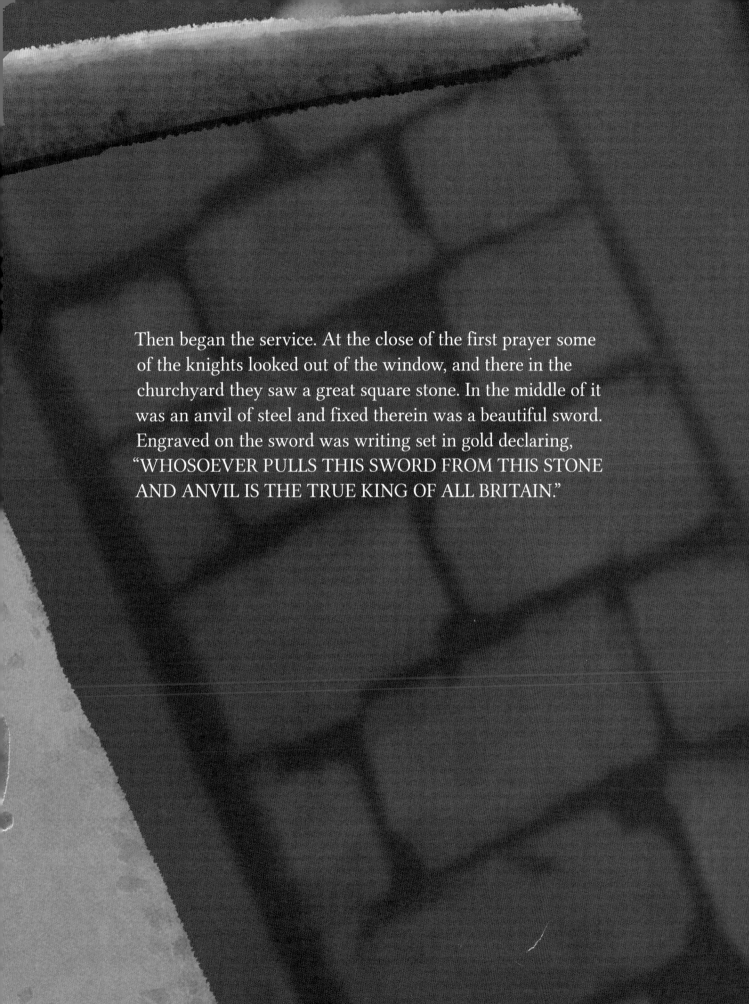

Then began the service. At the close of the first prayer some of the knights looked out of the window, and there in the churchyard they saw a great square stone. In the middle of it was an anvil of steel and fixed therein was a beautiful sword. Engraved on the sword was writing set in gold declaring, "WHOSOEVER PULLS THIS SWORD FROM THIS STONE AND ANVIL IS THE TRUE KING OF ALL BRITAIN."

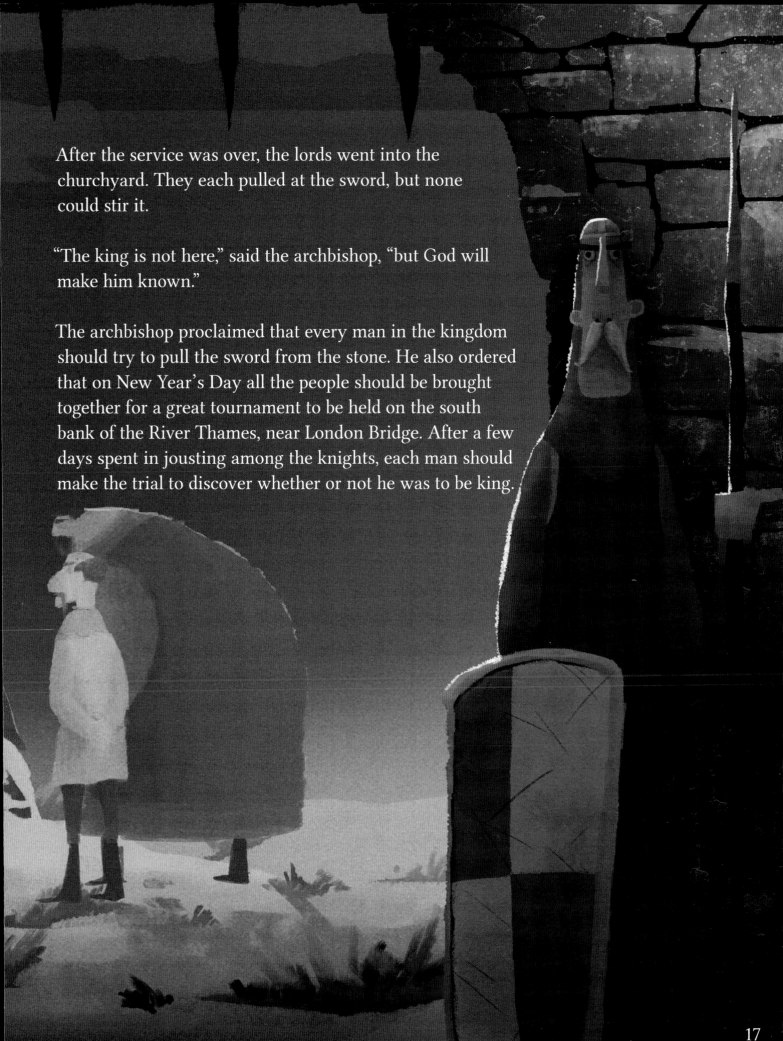

After the service was over, the lords went into the churchyard. They each pulled at the sword, but none could stir it.

"The king is not here," said the archbishop, "but God will make him known."

The archbishop proclaimed that every man in the kingdom should try to pull the sword from the stone. He also ordered that on New Year's Day all the people should be brought together for a great tournament to be held on the south bank of the River Thames, near London Bridge. After a few days spent in jousting among the knights, each man should make the trial to discover whether or not he was to be king.

Arthur did not know of the sword. Sir Ector had only told him *of* the tournament, but not the reason *for* the tournament. So in this way Arthur rode to London unaware of the importance of their journey.

As they entered the city, Sir Kay discovered he had left his sword at home. Distraught, he turned to his brother Arthur, "Will you go for my sword? I must have it to compete!"

"I shall with goodwill," said Arthur.

When Arthur returned to the castle, the drawbridge had been raised and he could not gain the warden's attention. Arthur decided, *I will hasten to the churchyard we passed and take the beautiful sword I saw in the stone. My brother Kay must have a weapon.*

He rode straight to the churchyard, dismounted, and strode toward the sword. Arthur pulled eagerly and the sword came with ease from the anvil.

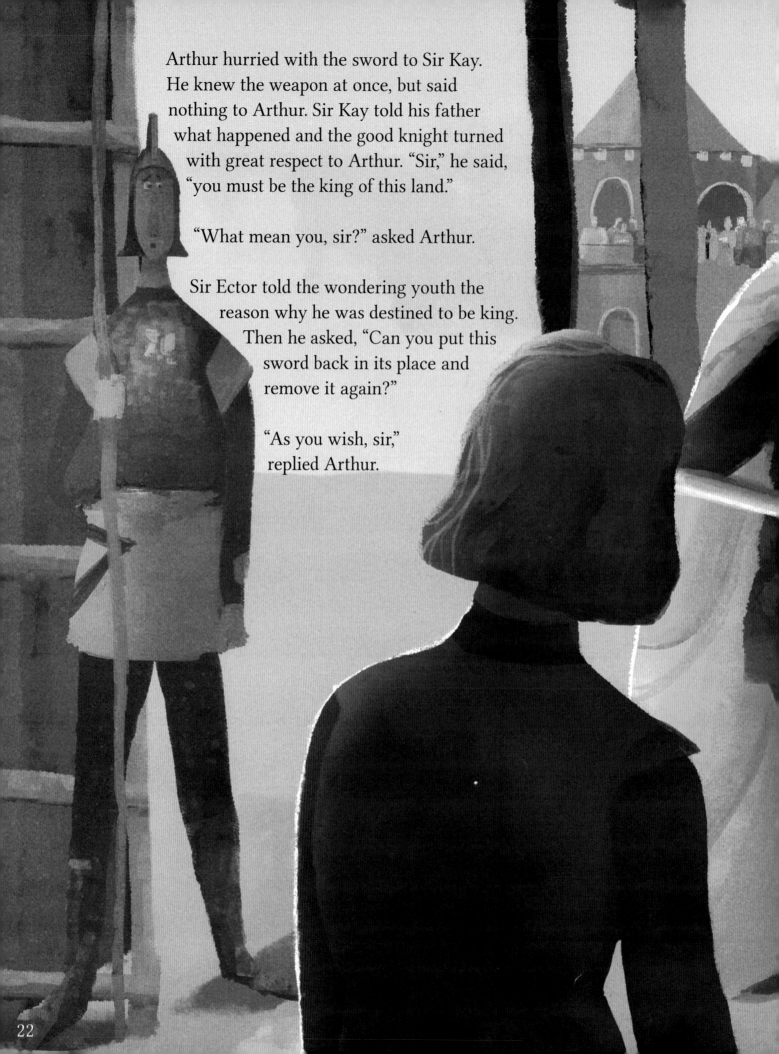

Arthur hurried with the sword to Sir Kay. He knew the weapon at once, but said nothing to Arthur. Sir Kay told his father what happened and the good knight turned with great respect to Arthur. "Sir," he said, "you must be the king of this land."

"What mean you, sir?" asked Arthur.

Sir Ector told the wondering youth the reason why he was destined to be king. Then he asked, "Can you put this sword back in its place and remove it again?"

"As you wish, sir," replied Arthur.

The three returned to the great stone and Arthur put the sword back as he had found it. Sir Ector tried to remove it but failed. "Now, you try," he said to Sir Kay, who in spite of his best efforts, also failed. Arthur, at Sir Ector's bidding, tried once again and successfully pulled forth the sword.

Sir Ector and Sir Kay immediately fell to their knees before Arthur.

"Alas," said Arthur, raising them from the ground, "my own dear father and my own dear brother, why do you kneel to me?"

"Nay, my Lord Arthur," said Sir Ector, "I am not your father."

"Long ago, when you were a baby, a mysterious man named Merlin brought you to me to be raised and cared for," explained Sir Ector. "He told me that you were the son of King Uther and Queen Igraine. He asked me to guard you in secrecy, lest your life be taken by the lords hoping to claim the throne."

Sir Ector continued, "I did not know whether the story was true or false, but you were a helpless child, so I took you in and brought you up as my own."

Arthur could not believe what he was hearing.

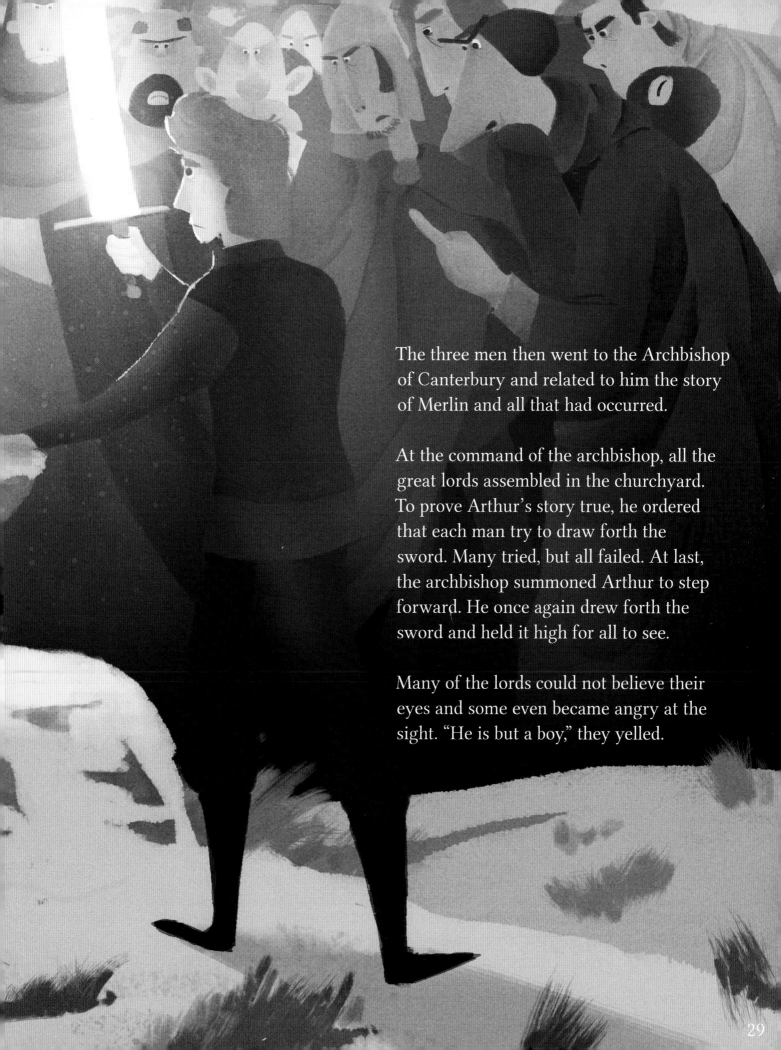

The three men then went to the Archbishop of Canterbury and related to him the story of Merlin and all that had occurred.

At the command of the archbishop, all the great lords assembled in the churchyard. To prove Arthur's story true, he ordered that each man try to draw forth the sword. Many tried, but all failed. At last, the archbishop summoned Arthur to step forward. He once again drew forth the sword and held it high for all to see.

Many of the lords could not believe their eyes and some even became angry at the sight. "He is but a boy," they yelled.

However, none could deny that Arthur was the rightful king. The townspeople fell to their knees exclaiming, "We will have Arthur as our king, for we see that it is God's will that he shall be our ruler."

The people, high and low, rich and poor, knelt to Arthur. He vowed that he would be a good and just king and the people vowed to serve and obey him. When he smiled kindly on them, they shouted joyfully: "Long live King Arthur! Long live the king!"

The newly crowned King Arthur immediately set about righting the wrongs done since the death of King Uther. He went on to fulfill a legacy unlike any that had come before him. To this day he is known as a great and honorable man. Many consider him the greatest king to have ever lived.